Written by Fariha

Illustrated by Fariha

Dedicated to my baby, Isa

There was a purple robot who
was playing with a ball.

Another red
robot came and
took his ball away.

Purple robot wanted to take it back but Red robot said, "Now it's mine, hahaha".

A much bigger robot came and he was black in color. He asked if they could all play together.

The Purple and Red Robots became very happy and they started playing together.

A blue robot watched them from far away and wanted to play.

The black robot noticed and went there and said, "Do you want to play?". Blue robot's face lit up and he said, "yes, yes , thank you so much!"

They all had so much fun together, sharing the ball with everyone.

It started to get dark and it was time to go home.

The Red robot wanted to take the ball with him.

But the purple robot stood up for himself and said "I am sorry, but this is mine and I will have to take it home".

The shy Blue robot said in a quiet voice, "yes we cannot take others' stuff".
The black robot said, "That's right! Always return what you borrow from other robots".

The red robot was a little sad to let go of the ball, but he understood that it was the right thing to do.

So he handed back the ball to the purple robot and the 4 robots became really good friends.

They would play hide and seek ....

...and many other games every afternoon in the same park happily ever after.

Remember:

Stand up for yourself, respect each
other and have fun together.

What is borrowed must be returned.

Sharing a toy and playing together can
be very fun!